C. S.

STO

FRIENDS
OF ACPL

3 1833 04424 3266

W9-BRL-236

ARTHUR THE KID

The gang was in trouble. They had just fouled up another bank robbery and, to make matters worse, they had accidentally given their real names to the bank manager! What was to be done? Well, first of all, they all changed their names; then they advertised for a tough boss, someone who would lead them on to greater deeds of crime.

They were all excited when a letter answering their ad arrived and it was signed by Billy the Kid, but when the gang went to meet the famed outlaw someone else showed up instead....

Who was that person and why did the gang wind up wearing women's dresses? What happened in a dark cave to make the outlaws faint, and why is this book named *Arthur the Kid?* All these questions and more are answered in this exciting and funny story.

THE ARTHUR BOOKS
Railroad Arthur
Arthur the Kid

ALAN COREN

ARTHUR THE KID

Illustrated by John Astrop

Little, Brown and Company
Boston   Toronto

COPYRIGHT © 1977 BY ALAN COREN

ALL RIGHTS RESERVED. NO PART OF THIS BOOK MAY BE REPRODUCED IN ANY FORM OR BY ANY ELECTRONIC OR MECHANICAL MEANS INCLUDING INFORMATION STORAGE AND RETRIEVAL SYSTEMS WITHOUT PERMISSION IN WRITING FROM THE PUBLISHER, EXCEPT BY A REVIEWER WHO MAY QUOTE BRIEF PASSAGES IN A REVIEW.

FIRST AMERICAN EDITION

T 03/78

Library of Congress Cataloging in Publication Data

Coren, Alan, 1938–
  Arthur the kid.

  SUMMARY: Ten-year-old Arthur the Kid takes over an outlaw gang and changes their lives forever.
  [1. The West—Fiction. 2. Robbers and outlaws—Fiction] I. Astrop, John. II. Title.
  PZ7.C81538Ar 1978   [Fic]   77-26989
  ISBN 0-316-15734-1

PRINTED IN THE UNITED STATES OF AMERICA

For Giles

★

874159

ONCE upon a time, about a hundred years ago, in a small mountain town in the middle of the territory of Wyoming, stood a bank.

The town was called Seminole Gap, and it was hardly surprising that it was a mountain town, since almost all the towns of Wyoming, even today, are mountain towns. For the Rockies, that two-thousand-mile chain of towering peaks that stretches down the length of western America from Canada almost to the Mexican border, pass right through Wyoming, and indeed fill three quarters of the state with some of the highest mountains of their range: mountains with fine, thrilling names like Cloud Peak, Grand Teton, Medicine Bow Peak, and Electric Peak. And past the feet of these run the rivers of Wyoming, fed with mountain

1

snow, blue, clean, cold rivers with fine names of their own: the Sweetwater River and the Bighorn River, the Powder River and the Cheyenne.

All of which now makes Wyoming one of the most magnificent states, but at the time I'm talking about, it also happened to be one of the most dangerous territories, because it was filled with the worst outlaws there were. Sometimes they were there just to hide in the mountains from the law, but more often it was up there, among the fine-sounding peaks, that they formed their terrible gangs to ride out and raid Wyoming itself, and the territories around it. For, being a mountainous territory, it was an easy place to disappear in and an easy place to strike from. The law, the sheriffs, the marshals, the posses could not search each tiny cleft in the rocks, climb each soaring mountainside, track down each villain to his hideout among the great gray slabs. There were even whole outlaw towns up there, close to the clouds, towns like Hole-in-the-Wall and Robbers Roost where no lawman dared go. They were full of every sort of armed, desperate, and murderous outlaw you could possibly imagine.

But Seminole Gap, named (in case you were wondering) after Wyoming's largest Indian tribe, was not that kind of town at all. It was a clean, quiet, rather sleepy town of perhaps a hundred or so white wooden houses, a dozen or so white wooden shops strung out along its single street, two white wooden churches — one with a spire and one without — a white wooden school, and a white wooden bank.

The bank looked pretty proud of itself, standing alone at the end of the street, with a white fence around it, a green lawn in front of it, and a flag on a white flagpole in the middle of the green lawn. It also had a big brass sign

3

announcing FIRST CITY BANK OF SEMINOLE GAP, which the bank clerk, Charlie Hoskins, had to polish every day, so brightly that the high mountains behind the little town were reflected in the brass plate as sharply as in a photograph.

That was the sort of attention to detail that the bank manager, Mr. Oliver Hickle, insisted on in everything. He was an extremely fussy man. He could not stand disorder or untidiness.

4

It was said, and there is no reason to believe that it wasn't true, that he stayed behind at the bank every night just to iron the dollar bills that people had paid in during the day. Every morning, when Charlie Hoskins turned up for work, he would say: "Good morning, Mr. Hickle, how's the money today?"

And every morning, Mr. Hickle would reply: "Nice and flat, Charlie, nice and flat!"

Not that ironing the money would have been too difficult a job; it wasn't a very busy bank, because it wasn't a very busy town. There was never very much money coming in, or going out.

Which was probably why, on that warm April morning, nobody in Seminole Gap paid any attention to the three men who rode their horses slowly down the street, reined in at the bank, and dismounted.

The townsfolk, it's true, glanced at them; it was, as I said, a small and quiet town, and strangers were consequently interesting and worth a glance, but no one looked closely. Even if they had, they probably wouldn't have

5

paid much attention to the fact that the three men had pretty terrifying faces under their three black hats, faces with dark eyes in them, dark beards on them, and scars all over them. They probably wouldn't have noticed either that each man wore his two six-guns low and

threateningly, or even that, as they walked into the bank, they pulled their grimy old kerchiefs up to cover their noses and mouths.

For the last thing the people of Seminole Gap were expecting was a robbery.

When he heard the three sets of spurs jangling across the bank floor, Charlie Hoskins looked up from behind his wire grille. He noticed the covered faces, but he just smiled and said: "Had a dusty ride, eh?"

The three men said nothing. They simply stepped up to the counter, and one of them pushed a note under the wire.

Charlie, puzzled, picked it up. When he read it, he was even more puzzled.

"This note," he said, "says that you all have buns."

The robbers looked at one another. The first one reached under the wire and snatched the note back.

"Thaggle a jiggle!" he shouted.

"What?" asked Charlie. "I can't hear. It's your scarf."

The robber pulled it down angrily.

"I said that's a *g!*" he yelled. "G for *gun!*"

"No, it's not," said Charlie. "A g is a loop with a tail that goes *down*. This" — here he pointed at the scrap of paper — "is a loop with a tail that goes *up*. It's a *b!*"

The second robber pulled his mask down, too, and his face was furious.

"You fool!" he yelled at the first one. "You said you could write!"

"Well, I can!" screamed the first one back. "Maybe I can't spell too good, but I can write. Look at all those words!"

The second robber snatched the piece of paper that the first was waving, tore it to bits, dropped the bits on the floor, and jumped up and down on them.

"Fat lot of good words are when they don't mean anything, when you come into a bank and say *Stick 'em up, I've got a bun!* It was your idea to write a note, so there wouldn't be any suspicious noises or anything, and now look, we've woken up half the town, and we've got our masks off, and . . ."

At which point, the commotion by now

being so rowdy, Mr. Oliver Hickle, the bank manager, ran in from his office.

"What on earth is going on?" he shrieked. He saw the bits of paper on the floor, and reeled back, shocked. "What's all that mess on my floor?"

"It's a note about buns, Mr. Hickle," said Charlie.

"NO IT ISN'T!" roared the first robber. "IT'S A NOTE ASKING FOR ALL THE MONEY IN THE BANK OR WE START SHOOTING!"

"I don't care what it's a note about," cried Mr. Hickle. "I'm not having filthy old rubbish lying around on my floor, this isn't a pigpen, you know, this happens to be a bank!"

"Thaggle woggle wiggle hergle," said the third robber, muffled.

"What?" shrieked Mr. Hickle. "What? I can't understand a word you say." He turned to Charlie. "If these are friends of yours, Hoskins, they can clear off right now, and you can clear off with them!"

So the third robber pulled his mask down, too.

"I SAID THAT'S WHY WE'RE HERE!" he yelled. "BECAUSE YOU'RE A BANK. WE'RE HERE BECAUSE YOU'RE A BANK, YOU OLD LOONY, AND WE HAVE COME TO ROB YOU!"

"SHUT UP!" shouted the first robber. "DO YOU WANT THE WHOLE TOWN TO HEAR?"

"WELL, *YOU'RE* SHOUTING!" howled the third man.

"*I'M* THE BOSS!" shrieked the first one.

"I beg your pardon," said Mr. Hickle, look-

3 1833 04424 3266

ing very offended. "*I* happen to be the bank manager. If there's any bossing to do, I shall be the one to do it. Now, who's going to pick up that paper?"

"RIGHT!" yelled the first robber. "That does it!"

And he pulled out his gun.

"Oh," said Mr. Hickle.

"Now," said the robber, "put all your money in this sack. One wrong move, my friend, and BING!"

"Bang, you idiot!" said the third robber. "They go bang, not bing. I've heard them."

Charlie Hoskins looked at the three men in some curiosity.

"Is this your first robbery?" he inquired.

"Never you mind that!" snapped the boss. "Just fill the sack from the safe!"

"If you say so," replied Charlie, and turned the huge wheel on the big brightly polished safe, and swung the door open. It was empty, except for one packet.

The robbers stared.

"Where's the money?" cried the boss.

"There isn't any," said Mr. Hickle, "I was just about to say."

The boss walked around the counter and grabbed the one packet from the safe.

"Those are my sandwiches," said Charlie Hoskins.

The second robber, who hadn't eaten that morning because he was too scared about what he had to do, suddenly cheered up.

"What kind?" he asked.

"Sardine and . . ."

"NEVER MIND WHAT KIND!" yelled the boss. "We haven't ridden fifty miles and risked getting shot and everything just to steal a rotten packet of sandwiches." He waved his six-gun at Mr. Hickle. "Now, for the last time, where's the money?"

Mr. Hickle sighed, and went to Charlie's drawer, and opened it. There were seven dollar bills in it, all beautifully pressed, and some small change. He put it on the counter.

"There you are," he said.

"*Seven bucks?*" gasped the boss.

"And eighty-four cents," said Mr. Hickle,

who was always very precise, especially where money was concerned.

The second robber turned bitterly on the boss.

"You've done it again!" he cried. "I'm sick and tired of you fouling things up! You said this bank was full of money, you said we wouldn't be able to carry away a half of what they had, and now look at it. We haven't got enough to make it worth bringing a sack; you could put the entire haul in your hat and not even notice!"

"It's got a flag on a flagpole, it's got a big brass plate," muttered the boss; "it looks just like the sort of bank to be stuffed with money."

"Thank you," said Mr. Hickle, who was, though he would never have admitted it, rather pleased to be robbed. The people of Seminole Gap might take him more seriously now they saw that he ran a bank worth robbing.

"Shut up!" shouted the boss. "What kind of a bank manager do you call yourself, nothing in the safe but sandwiches?"

"And what kind of a gang do you call *your-*

13

self," replied Charlie Hoskins, who wasn't going to stand by and hear people being rude to his employer, "choosing a bank with only seven dollars in it?"

"We're the Black Hand Gang, that's who!" cried the third robber. "And don't you forget it!"

"Oh, well done!" sneered the boss. "Why don't you give him our address as well?"

"We'll have to change our name again, now," muttered the second robber gloomily. "We're running out of things to call ourselves."

They might all have stood there all day, shouting accusations at one another, if at that moment the third robber had not glanced through the window.

"Hey, there's a mob coming!" he shouted. "Let's get out of here!"

The boss stuck his gun into Mr. Hickle's chest.

"Is there a back way out?" he snapped.

"Good thinking!" said the second robber.

"Yes," said Mr. Hickle, pointing.

The three robbers ran through the back door, after, it must be said, some pretty undignified jostling in the narrow doorway.

Less than a minute later, they were jostling back in again.

"Left the horses out the front," explained the third robber, as he ran past Charlie Hoskins.

The Black Hand Gang rushed out of the front door this time, leaped onto their horses, and rode away just as the crowd, led by the sheriff, arrived at the fence, realized what was going on, and started shooting.

But, never having had a robbery before and consequently having had little practice with guns, they missed everything except the boss's hat, which flew from his head like a great black crow as the gang galloped out of Seminole Gap.

It was the first stroke of luck the gang had had all day.

The Black Hand Gang sat in a small smelly cave, high in the mountains, twenty miles from Seminole Gap, wondering what to do next.

"Imagine leaving the money behind," said

the boss bitterly. "I could have bought a new hat with that seven dollars."

"*And* we forgot our sack," said the second robber.

"It's been an expensive day, all things considered," said the third. "Not to mention having to change our name again. It'll be the third time in a month."

"I liked the Railroad Mob best," said the boss. "It had a nice ring to it. Professional."

"We could still be called that," replied the second robber, "if you hadn't fouled up that train ambush."

"How was I to know the train didn't stop at Yellow Creek?"

"I don't think you're supposed to ambush them at *stations*," said the third robber. "You're supposed to stick a log across the line in the middle of nowhere, and when they stop, you jump on and rob them. I felt silly, standing around on that platform with my gun out, just watching the train go through. And then *he* made things even worse," and here he pointed at the second robber, "by refusing to buy

17

tickets on the grounds that we were the Rail-road Mob. Not to mention where I got shot in the boot as we escaped."

"I did think up the next name, though," said the second outlaw. "You all liked the Three Rustlers. It had a kind of neat simplicity."

"If you'd told us you were afraid of cows," said the boss, nastily, "it would have helped too, wouldn't it? We did a very good operation that time, got the cattle away in the middle of the night, none of the cowboys woke up, and then you had to go and scream."

"It mooed at me," said the second robber quietly. "It looked like a bull in the moonlight, and I thought: it's going to run at me."

"Anyway," said the third outlaw, "what shall we call ourselves now? Everybody will be looking for the Black Hand Gang; *and* laughing about it, which is worse."

"I reckon," said the boss, "that we ought to pick individual names this time. Really good frightening ones. I have been thinking about it for some time, and I'm going to be the Seminole Kid."

"There's one already," the second robber objected. "He might not like someone else coming along and using his name."

"So what?"

"Nothing, except he's got an iron hook where his left hand used to be, and he carries a shotgun with fourteen notches on it, and I once saw him bite a man's ear off in Laramie just for asking him the time."

"Oh," said the boss. "All right, I'll be Seminole Maurice."

"That's a good idea," said the third outlaw, "we'll use our own names, it'll help us remember. I'll be the Charles B. Sutcliffe Kid."

"That's ridiculous. It sounds all wrong. *I'll* decide our names, being boss. You're Murderous B. Sutcliffe, and you" — Seminole Maurice turned to the second robber — "can be Fat Phil."

"But I'm thin."

"Exactly!" cried Seminole Maurice. "Can you think of a better way to confuse the law?"

Fat Phil thought for a long while, and couldn't, so they all wrote their names on their gun handles with their knives, so they wouldn't forget.

They all felt better, after that.

"Okay," said Seminole Maurice, "here's my plan."

The other two cheered up even more. Plans, it must be said, were their favorite part of the whole operation. They always sounded so brilliant; they always looked so possible, sketched out with a stick in the dust, with everyone being briefed on his particular job. Plans were really exciting. If only they didn't have to be carried out, there would be no problems.

"I reckon," said Seminole Maurice, "that we ought to hold up stagecoaches. They're slower than trains, they're not locked like banks, and they won't go moo and frighten the life out of Fat Phil. Also, they have only one guard. It's a cinch!"

"How do you get them to stop?" inquired Fat Phil. "I'm not standing around on any more platforms, like a fool."

"There's nothing like that," snapped Seminole Maurice. "We'll find out when a stagecoach is due to come down the trail, then we'll ride out and block the road, the stagecoach will stop, and we'll just sort of, well, rob it."

"Will we have to shoot anybody?" asked Murderous B. Sutcliffe, a trifle uneasily.

"Of course not," replied Seminole Maurice. "We'll rely on surprise. They'll be so shocked to see us, they'll just surrender. After all, we look pretty terrible. We're just about the ugliest gang I ever saw. Sometimes I catch sight of us as we're walking past a shop window, and it scares the life out of me."

"I wouldn't say I was so ugly," said Murderous B. Sutcliffe. "I think I have a rather interesting face."

"Ho yes, that's for sure!" cried Fat Phil scornfully. "It's so interesting, the first time my horse saw it, he wouldn't eat for three days!"

"Just shut up, the pair of you," barked Seminole Maurice, who, now he had a plan again, was feeling once more like a boss. "We're going to have to hold up a stage tomorrow, if we want to eat, so let's get some sleep and start out early."

"Eat," murmured Fat Phil, his terrible eyes glazing, "we haven't had food for two days."

"Not since we tried to run out of that restaurant in Poker Bend without paying," said Murderous B. Sutcliffe, "only you caught your spur in the tablecloth and pulled the whole thing down, and we had to pay for three plates and a vase of flowers as well as the meal, and that was our last five dollars."

"Well, we'll eat tomorrow, all right," said Seminole Maurice, and they all curled up with their heads on their saddles. The sun sank low over the Rockies, spilling gold down their great gray flanks and turning the sky beyond the little cave mouth to pale fire; the world fell silent into night, save for the low, sad rumbling of three empty stomachs, echoing in the dark.

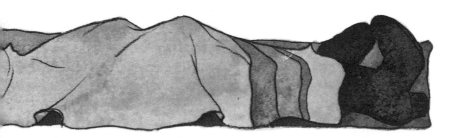

The three outlaws sat square in their saddles, squinting down the mountain trail into the blue morning mist.

"It'll be along any minute now," said Seminole Maurice. "The Rock Springs stage always passes this way just one hour after sunup. With any luck, it'll be carrying gold!"

"With any luck," muttered Fat Phil, "the guard'll still be asleep."

"Never mind about the guard!" snapped Seminole Maurice. "Just concentrate on keeping your horse plumb in the middle of the trail. Standing this way, three abreast, we're occupying the whole road, and there's a sheer drop to one side, and a sheer cliff straight up from the other. We got 'em cold, boys!"

Murderous B. Sutcliffe suddenly held up his hand.

"I think I hear something!" he hissed.

They listened. Far off, invisible hooves thudded, unseen wheels rasped.

They pulled up their kerchiefs. They drew out their guns. They peered into the mist. They held their breath. The noise of hoof and wheel grew louder.

It turned to thunder!

It filled their ears!

And, suddenly, exploding out of the eddying whorls of mist, the Rock Springs stagecoach, like some fearful four-headed, sixteen-legged monster, burst upon them!

And among them!

And through them!

And vanished, squealing and grinding and rocking, around the bend.

Seminole Maurice was the first to pick himself up. He was covered with dust and had swallowed a tooth. His left leg hurt terribly where a coach wheel had run over it, and his shirt was torn. As the dust settled, he became aware of Murderous B. Sutcliffe, who was about six feet off the ground, hanging onto a tree root protruding from the sheer cliff face, and minus both boots.

Of Fat Phil, there was no sign at all.

"They didn't stop," wheezed Murderous B. Sutcliffe, coughing dust.

"Road hogs!" cried Seminole Maurice. "It's people like that cause all the accidents!"

"Speaking as an accident," said Murderous B. Sutcliffe, dropping from his branch, and becoming a heap on the road, "I blame my horse. It just reared up out of the way. Luckily, I grabbed that root in time. How about you?"

"Mine did, too," muttered Seminole Maurice, rubbing his injured leg. "Just went up on its hind legs, threw me off, and — where *are* the horses, anyway?"

Murderous B. Sutcliffe looked around. The morning sun was burning off the mist now, but it didn't help.

"Run off," he said. "More to the point, where's Fat Phil?"

Seminole Maurice looked glum.

"There's only one place he *could* be," he replied, nodding toward the sheer drop.

The two outlaws walked, or rather limped, to the terrible edge, and looked down. A mile below, the silver thread that was the Yellowstone River flashed back the bright sunlight. Of Fat Phil, there was, naturally by now, no sign.

"I feel sick," said Murderous B. Sutcliffe.

They both sat down at the other side of the road, trying not to think about Fat Phil, or how long it would have taken him to reach the bottom of the canyon, or what he might have thought about on the long way down. They were hurt, miserable, disappointed, hungry, and so lost in their own miseries that they did not hear the hooves coming slowly toward them, up the trail.

"Here's another fine mess you've got us into!" cried a familiar voice.

They looked up.

"Fat Phil!" they cried.

"Or what's left of him," muttered Fat Phil, who was gray with dust and sticky with sweat and gasping for breath. So was his horse.

"We thought you were dead!" cried Seminole Maurice.

"Might as well be," replied Fat Phil. "I may never ride a horse again."

"Why ever not?" asked Murderous B. Sutcliffe.

"You wouldn't ask why not," said Fat Phil,

28

"if *you'd* been chased five miles down a mountain trail by a four-horse stagecoach!"

"How did that happen?" asked Seminole Maurice.

Fat Phil glared at him furiously.

"Well may you ask!" he cried. "It was your rotten plan, after all! Stand in the way, you said; the stagecoach will stop, you said! No plans for what might happen if it didn't, were there? No plans for how to deal with my horse not wishing to be run down by the stage and just galloping off in front of it. Some plan! Some *boss!*"

"Don't go on," groaned Seminole Maurice; "everybody makes mistakes."

"They don't make 'em every day!" snapped Fat Phil. "Especially when they're supposed to be bosses and leaders and everything."

Murderous B. Sutcliffe, still squatting in the dust, nodded.

"I don't mean this in a nasty way," he said to Seminole Maurice, "but I think someone else ought to be boss."

"I agree," said Fat Phil.

"So do I," said Seminole Maurice. "I'm sick of everyone shouting at me. Which of you wants to be boss?"

Neither of them said anything.

"Now what?" inquired Seminole Maurice.

"Let's get someone else to be boss," suggested Fat Phil. "Can't we employ someone to do it?"

"You can't employ someone to be boss," said Murderous B. Sutcliffe. "It's the wrong way round. It's bosses that employ people."

"Not necessarily," said Seminole Maurice. "There must be lots of bosses looking for gangs to lead. It's just a question of finding them. Know what I think?"

"There's another rotten idea coming," muttered Fat Phil gloomily.

"*I* think," Seminole Maurice persisted, ig-

30

noring him, "that we ought to put an ad in the Medicine Bow paper. In the *Help Wanted.* We won't give our names or anything, otherwise the law'll be onto us, we'll just say 'Tough gang seeks boss, please write stating name and qualifications,' and we'll put a box number down, which is just a number people have to put on the envelope they send to the newspaper. We can go in and collect the letter and nobody need ever know who put the ad in. It can't fail!" he ended triumphantly.

"I've heard that before," said Fat Phil, who was still feeling bitter. "And it always fails."

"Well, I reckon we ought to try it," said Murderous B. Sutcliffe, "so you're outvoted."

"Right!" cried Seminole Maurice, whose new plan had at least cheered *him* up considerably. "Let's dash down to Medicine Bow right away."

"Not going to be much dashing," said Fat Phil, "with three of us on one horse."

They all climbed onto Fat Phil's horse, and the horse's legs buckled a bit, and he whinnied a bit, but he reckoned that it was all part of a horse's life, and he took a deep breath, and, clutching each other for support, the three outlaws set out, very carefully and wobbling slightly, for Medicine Bow.

"I can't believe it!" said Murderous B. Sutcliffe, for the fourth time that day. "Can I see the letter again?"

Seminole Maurice handed him the piece of paper.

Murderous B. Sutcliffe opened it for the fourth time, and cleared his throat for the fourth time.

"*Regarding your vacant position for a tough boss,*" he read aloud, "*I should like to apply for the job. As to qualifications, there is no one tougher, you can ask anybody. If you are still*

interested, meet me behind the hollow tree at the fork on the Pig's Ear trail. Signed," and here Murderous B. Sutcliffe paused dramatically for the fourth time, *"Billy the Kid!"*

They had collected the letter that morning from the office of the Medicine Bow newspaper, just three days after putting in their advertisement. At first, they had been extremely excited, and had jumped up and down in the street at this amazing stroke of luck.

But, after they had calmed down, they had thought about it, and become just a tiny bit worried. They had, of course, already heard about Billy the Kid, whose full name was William H. Bonney and who was known throughout the West as a very tough man indeed. This was what worried them. Billy the Kid's hobby, they had heard, was not stamp collecting, and it was not train watching, and it was not breeding white mice: Billy the Kid's hobby was shooting people. It was rumored that he had shot twenty-eight men, though some said he had shot as many as fifty, and some said even Billy the Kid didn't know how many he had shot, since his counting wasn't nearly as good as his shooting.

"I hope he likes us," Fat Phil had said. "If he doesn't like us, we could end up as three more notches on his gun. I think we should have put something in the ad about the boss having to like us."

"I just hope we're good enough for him," Murderous B. Sutcliffe had said, nervously. "When I think what he would have done if he'd been with us at the Seminole Gap Bank, I feel sick." He had turned to glare at Seminole Maurice. "I just hope this isn't going to turn out to be another of your rotten horrible plans."

"Rubbish!" cried Seminole Maurice, "It's a marvelous plan! We're going to ride with Billy the Kid. It's a terrific plan!"

But all the same, when he said it, he had looked a little pale, and he had felt a little funny inside.

34

The day had passed, as days do, and the sun had begun to set behind the fork on the Pig's Ear trail specified in Billy the Kid's note. He had not appeared all day, and the three outlaws assumed he would be coming that night. Although they were looking forward to meeting him, as the night crept on, and the sky grew darker, and the shadow of the hollow tree stretched longer and longer, and the Wyoming coyotes began to howl eerily in the towering mountains, the three could not stop themselves from shivering.

Suddenly, the last blazing rim of sun fell below the peaks, and night, as it will in those altitudes, came quickly on.

They were in the dark, waiting for the most dangerous gunman in the West!

Their eyes strained.

Their ears stretched.

874159

Nothing.

Until —

"*What's that?*" hissed Fat Phil.

A heel rasped on the gritty trail!

"DON'T SHOOT!" shrieked Murderous B. Sutcliffe.

"Shut up, you fool!" snapped Seminole Maurice.

"Who's there?" said a voice, and it was not one of their voices.

"Nobody!" cried Murderous B. Sutcliffe, whose nerves were by now completely shredded. "We're all somewhere else!"

"No we're not," said Seminole Maurice, who was braver than the other two, though not much. "We're here. Is that Billy the Kid?"

"Yes," said the voice.

"I'm going to be sick," whispered Fat Phil.

"Pull yourself together!" said Seminole

Maurice sharply. He nudged his horse toward the sound of the strange voice. "Good evening, Billy the Kid. I am Seminole Maurice, and there are two people here in the dark with me, called Fat Phil and Murderous B. Sutcliffe. If you will follow us to our hideout, we shall introduce ourselves properly."

"All right," said the voice, and the three outlaws peered into the blackness, but could still make out nothing but the vaguest of outlines, "lead on. But go slowly; I haven't got a horse."

"It isn't far," said Seminole Maurice, and they all set off for the cave.

It took about twenty minutes to reach the cave, during which time nobody said anything at all (although Fat Phil, it must be said, whimpered once or twice when he began to think of all the things that might go wrong). When they arrived, the three outlaws dismounted, and Seminole Maurice went inside, and lit a couple of candles, and the shadows flickered in the thin yellow light. The three of them licked their lips nervously, and waited,

until Seminole Maurice took a deep breath and called, "Come on in!"

"Sir!" hissed Murderous B. Sutcliffe. "Call him sir!"

"Come on in, sir!"

And through the black cavemouth, as if through a velvet curtain, a figure stepped; and, having stepped, stood, blinking at the unaccustomed light.

The outlaws stared!

38

The outlaws gaped!

The outlaws could not believe their eyes!

For the figure standing in front of them was a small boy, about ten years old!

Who was also looking at *them* in some surprise.

It was Seminole Maurice who found his voice first, though not without difficulty.

"Are *you*," he croaked, "Billy the Kid?"

"Yes," said the small boy.

Seminole Maurice swallowed.

"Excuse me," he said, "would you mind if I had a word in private with my associates?"

"Not at all," said the small boy, who was clearly very polite, especially for the most dangerous killer in the West.

The three outlaws retreated to the back of the cave.

"There's got to be some mistake," muttered Seminole Maurice. "He's just a kid!"

"He wouldn't be called Billy the Kid if he wasn't," whispered Fat Phil, with some logic.

"Don't be ridiculous!" snapped Murderous B. Sutcliffe. "Billy the Kid isn't *that* sort of kid. He's only called the Kid because he's young and small."

"Well, *this* one's young and small," replied Fat Phil, who was really having quite a sensible evening, for him.

"This one's a *child*," hissed Seminole Maurice. "And not only does he not have a gun, he isn't even big enough to hold one! Are you trying to tell us that we are looking at someone who has shot twenty-eight people, or possibly fifty?"

"It's going to be tricky finding out," said Fat Phil. "If we ask him whether he's a child, and he isn't, he could start shooting, and we'd just be three more notches on his gun. I mean, imagine if you were a very small man and people went around asking you if you were a child, you'd get pretty angry, wouldn't you? That could be why he's killed so many people. Did you ever think of that?"

"He hasn't *got* a gun," said Murderous B. Sutcliffe.

"Maybe it's in that carpetbag he's carrying," said Seminole Maurice. "Maybe he can undo a carpetbag like greased lightning."

"*I've* got an idea," said Fat Phil. "Why don't we ask him what his full name is? If he says it's William H. Bonney, we'll know for sure."

"Good thinking!" cried Seminole Maurice.

They came out of their huddle and approached the boy.

"Excuse me, sir," said Seminole Maurice,

who was still taking no chances. "We have told you our full names, I wondered if you'd mind telling us yours?"

"All right," said the small boy. "I am Arthur William Foskett."

"HA!" shouted Seminole Maurice. "Then you are not Billy the Kid!"

"My middle name is Billy for short," said the small boy, "and I am a kid."

"You're not *the* Billy the Kid, though," said Fat Phil. "You should have signed your letter *Arthur* the Kid, to avoid confusion."

"If you think it's confusing," said the boy, "then I'll *be* Arthur the Kid."

"It's a bit late for that," said Seminole Maurice bitterly. "Why did you answer the ad anyway? You're a child. How can you lead a tough gang, that's what I'd like to know?"

"It's not my fault," said Arthur the Kid, "I was as surprised as you were. I thought you were going to be a gang of boys. You should have said you were grown-ups in the advertisement. And I'm very good at leading gangs, even if I do say so myself. I can make maps, and

42

track, and tie every sort of knot there ever was. I can make a fire by rubbing sticks together; I can lead expeditions, climb any tree you point at, and I have better ideas for games than anyone you ever met. And in this carpetbag I've got all kinds of important gang things, like rope, a compass, a magnifying glass, signal flags, a frying pan, and a knife with eight blades. We could have a lot of fun, even if you are a bit old."

"He's right, you know," said Fat Phil. "I've always wanted to go on an expedition. Maybe we could find the North Pole."

"Oh, shut up!" shouted Seminole Maurice. "Our job is robbing banks and ambushing trains and holding up stagecoaches, not looking for Poles."

Arthur the Kid looked at them.

"I had the feeling you were outlaws," he said. "I bet you're not much good at it, either, otherwise you wouldn't be living in this smelly old cave and looking for a boss. I bet you haven't got the first idea how to be an outlaw."

You will have noticed that Arthur the Kid had stopped being as polite as he had been at the start. This was because he didn't see much point in being polite with criminals.

"Just you keep quiet," said Seminole Maurice ominously, "if you know what's good for you. You're in enough trouble as it is. We're going to have to decide what to do with you."

"We can't let him go," said Murderous B. Sutcliffe. "He knows our new names, and he knows what we look like, and he knows where our hideout is."

"I *knew* this was going to be another one of your rotten ideas," said Fat Phil gloomily. "I *said* it would be."

Seminole Maurice took out his gun. The candlelight winked off the bright barrel. He spun the chamber, and the clicking was a terrible sound.

"We ought to shoot him," he said, "right now."

44

Arthur the Kid looked at him, very straight,
and not afraid. He was as brave as it is possible
to be.

"But we won't, will we?" said Murderous B.
Sutcliffe.

"Why not?" snapped Seminole Maurice.

"Because we're not like that," said Fat Phil.
Seminole Maurice sighed.

"You're right," he said. He holstered his gun.
"I wish we were, though. Because if we can't

send him back, and if we can't shoot him, he'll have to ride with us. It's the only way."

"I'm not riding with a gang of criminals," said Arthur the Kid loudly. "I'm not going round the country taking things that don't belong to me."

"You'll do what you're told!" snapped Seminole Maurice.

Fat Phil suddenly threw a pebble at the wall, angrily.

"Rotten plan, I said," he muttered, "and rotten plan, I meant! We're worse off than ever. At least this morning there were only three of us who had no idea how to be outlaws. Now there's four of us. There'd be even less food to go around, if we had any, which we haven't."

"I've got some frankfurters," said Arthur the Kid.

The three terrible bearded heads turned to stare at him.

"Frankfurters?" whispered Murderous B. Sutcliffe.

"You collect some brushwood," said Arthur

46

the Kid, "and I'll get my frying pan and things ready."

Five minutes later, in the warm flicker of firelight and the rich lip-smacking aroma of sizzled wieners, the three outlaws and Arthur the Kid sat forking down the supper of which the robbers had been dreaming for two days.

"Maybe it wasn't such a rotten idea, after all," said Fat Phil, as he swallowed, eyes closed, the last piece of fried bread from the loaf which Arthur the Kid had also had the foresight to pack.

Speak for yourself, thought Arthur the Kid. But he didn't say anything. He was going to wait and see.

He was the first to wake on the following morning, as the day's new sunlight fell warm on his face. He would have got up and gone out of the cave to do his special exercises, which he did every morning without fail, had it not been for the fact that Seminole Maurice had tied

47

himself to Arthur the Kid with a chain and padlock.

So he rolled onto his back and stared up at the roof of the cave, and did some hard thinking.

He knew he could probably find a way of escaping from the gang; they weren't very bright, and they didn't work things out in advance, and he knew an opportunity would present itself for him to slip away from them. But that wouldn't solve the problem which he was beginning to realize he had; for the fact was that Arthur the Kid really rather liked the three outlaws. After supper the night before, they had all talked a lot and told him about how they had decided to become outlaws because they weren't any good at anything else they had tried; and he had seen for himself that they weren't really wicked at all, just a little unlucky and a little dumb.

But the snag was that they *were* outlaws; which meant that if he did escape, then he was bound to go to the sheriff and tell him the whole story. Arthur the Kid was not a tattle-

48

tale; it was simply that if someone didn't stop them, the three outlaws might commit crimes against innocent people, hurt someone, or, most likely of all, get hurt themselves, or put in prison, and Arthur the Kid hated the idea of Seminole Maurice or Murderous B. Sutcliffe or Fat Phil getting shot or stuck in jail for years and years.

The only thing to do, he decided that morning, was to stay with them and find a way of saving them from a life of crime. After all, so far they hadn't really done anything *too* terrible: they had *tried,* but they had failed. They had no money that didn't belong to them; they had never fired a gun at anyone. If they could be stopped from getting into any more trouble, the law would probably let them off with a few sharp words.

That was provided Arthur the Kid *could* stop them from getting into any real trouble; and also persuade them to turn over a new leaf and give up wanting to be criminals.

It wasn't going to be easy. He realized that when Seminole Maurice rolled over suddenly, tugging him on the chain, and woke up shouting.

"That's it!" he cried, so loudly that Fat Phil and Murderous B. Sutcliffe were startled awake, too, and (thinking the cave was under attack from the law) went for their guns. Which might have been very dangerous for everybody in it, except that they couldn't remember where they'd put them.

"What's up?" shouted Murderous B. Sutcliffe, rummaging desperately through his saddlebags.

"I've just had the most amazing dream," replied Seminole Maurice. "I saw the whole thing before me!"

"Which whole thing?" asked Fat Phil.

Arthur the Kid just listened, saying nothing.

Seminole Maurice unlocked the chain so that he could leap up and throw his arms around enthusiastically.

"Our next job, that's what!" he said. "I dreamed we held up the Wells, Fargo office in Fort Halleck!"

Now, it was clear from Seminole Maurice's excitement that he expected everyone else to throw their hats in the air and cheer and generally give him the support he felt his dream so richly deserved.

But all he got was a dull thud.

"What was that?" he said, spinning round.

"It was Fat Phil," replied Murderous B. Sutcliffe. "He's fainted."

Arthur the Kid, knowing that the other two wouldn't have the first idea what to do, ran across and, with Murderous B. Sutcliffe's help, dragged Fat Phil out into the fresh morning air, loosened his collar, then sat him up and pushed his head down between his knees. After a few seconds, Fat Phil came to.

"What happened?" said Seminole Maurice.

Fat Phil looked at him.

"You have had some rotten plans in your time," he said, "and you have had some silly plans, and some crazy plans, too. But this is a historic day, Seminole Maurice. Because today you have had your first rotten, silly, *and* crazy plan!"

"He's right," said Murderous B. Sutcliffe. "The Wells, Fargo office is just about the best-guarded building in the entire world!"

It was true. Wells, Fargo & Company had been set up in the 1860s just because the other stagecoach lines that carried valuable goods across America were constantly being attacked by outlaws and Indians. Particularly after the great gold rush of the middle of the century, it had become virtually impossible to guarantee that a gold shipment would get through to its destination. So Wells, Fargo had gone into business with specially armored coaches, specially trained teams of crack drivers and crack shots, and introduced a system of having stages accompanied by armed escorts who rode in front and behind. They had also turned their staging posts into small forts.

And the stage line that ran through southern Wyoming was especially well guarded, because it ran up from Colorado and into Utah and it carried the huge shipments of silver and gold that were being taken every day from the rich mines of Colorado. Fort Bridger and Fort Halleck were the Wyoming staging posts, where the horses were changed, and the Fort Halleck post alone was guarded by twelve of Wells, Fargo's toughest officers.

So you can see why Fat Phil fainted.

"Cowards!" yelled Seminole Maurice. "You're all cowards!"

Now, whatever else they might have been, the other two outlaws certainly didn't think of themselves as cowards, and Seminole Maurice's insult stung them. Which was probably why Murderous B. Sutcliffe made the big mistake of saying "All right, then, let's hear this plan of yours."

"That's better," said Seminole Maurice. "I suppose it was the surprise of meeting Arthur the Kid, or being chained to him or something, which did it, because I dreamed about him. I dreamed about us having this boy with us, and how we would manage, and it sort of came to me in the dream that we would be able to use him just *because* he was a small boy. There we were, walking into the Wells, Fargo office, just an ordinary family with a father and a boy and a mother and an old granny. Because the whole trick with robbing a Wells, Fargo office is getting inside, past the guards; once you're in, it's easy. So, as soon as we were inside — where the gold was stacked, waiting for the stage — we whipped out our guns, held up the cashier, got him to fill our saddlebags with gold bars, and then tied him up and rode off. Fort Halleck's only ten miles from some of the wildest mountain country in the whole state, in an hour we were so lost they didn't even know where to start looking."

It was Fat Phil who spoke first. "All right, just suppose we went along with it, where do we get a mother and a granny from? We've only got Arthur the Kid so far."

Murderous B. Sutcliffe looked at him scornfully. "He means us, you idiot! We'll dress up."

"*What?*" cried Fat Phil. "I didn't become an outlaw to go around in a skirt! You don't see Jesse James or Butch Cassidy or the Dalton Gang mincing around in high heels and lipstick!"

"And that," said Seminole Maurice triumphantly, "is exactly why none of those so-called top outlaws has ever managed to rob Wells, Fargo!" His eyes glazed dreamily. "We'll be the most famous gang of all time," he murmured. "They'll tell stories to their grandchildren about us, they'll write songs about us, our faces will be on reward posters everywhere."

Well, the other two were a bit stupid, and Arthur the Kid had reasons, as we know, for not interfering, so that when Fat Phil and Murderous B. Sutcliffe got to thinking about how famous they would be, they really couldn't resist Seminole Maurice's plan after all. It might just work, they thought to themselves, and if it did, oh, if it did . . .

Which was why, just half an hour later and

having eaten the last of Arthur the Kid's frankfurters for breakfast, they saddled up and set off to ride the sixty miles to Fort Halleck.

Arthur the Kid rode behind Fat Phil, holding onto his gunbelt, and thought very hard indeed.

"How do I look?" said Murderous B. Sutcliffe.

They were on the gravely bank of the Green River, only five miles from Fort Halleck, just before noon on the following day. Early that morning, they had passed through the little town of Rock Springs, and it was from a garden there that Murderous B. Sutcliffe and Fat Phil had snatched the dresses they were both now wearing. It had been their first ever successful crime, but even then, and simple as it was to steal things drying on a clothesline, they had nearly brought disaster on themselves by hanging around in the garden and arguing about which of them was to be the granny. At last, it had been satisfactorily decided; and now Murderous B. Sutcliffe, in a green gingham dress, paraded before the others as Arthur's fake mother.

"Not bad," said Seminole Maurice, "but pull the bonnet down a bit."

Arthur the Kid sighed.

"There *is* just one other thing," he said, "I think he ought to shave his beard off."

"Good thinking," said Seminole Maurice. "I was trying to work out why he didn't look quite right."

Fat Phil and Murderous B. Sutcliffe both went down to the river's edge to shave, and when they returned, Arthur the Kid was surprised at what nice kindly faces they had. In fact, when Fat Phil climbed into his pink flowered dress, Arthur the Kid thought he made a really rather charming old granny. Though he didn't, of course, point this out.

So they all remounted, and, hearts beating more than a little, began the last stage of their ride. Naturally, Fat Phil and Murderous B. Sutcliffe looked a trifle peculiar — two ladies with their skirts up around their waists and

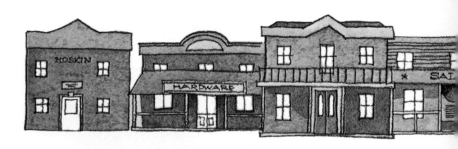

dirty old trousers and big black boots hanging
down on either side of their horses — but they
reckoned on not meeting anyone along the
trail. When they reached the edge of Fort Halleck, which was hardly a town at all, just the
Wells, Fargo office and a saloon and a few little
buildings, these two dismounted with Arthur
the Kid, and left Seminole Maurice to ride in
with the horses and tie them up to the rail outside the office, according to plan.

And it was just as they were about to put the
plan into operation (Fat Phil and Murderous B.
Sutcliffe were straightening their skirts and
pulling their bonnets down to hide as much of
their faces as possible) that Arthur the Kid,
being by far the most observant of the four of

them, noticed something really quite extraordinary.

"Do you realize," he said, "that there is nobody in Fort Halleck at all?"

The other three stared.

It was true.

It was the middle of the day, and there was smoke rising from the red tin chimney of the saloon, and a fire glowing in the darkness of the blacksmith's forge next door to the Wells, Fargo office; there were horses tied up to various rails, and a stagecoach waiting in the dusty little street, but of human beings — cowboys, guards, drivers, blacksmiths, passengers, townsfolk — there was absolutely no sign.

"Now," murmured Arthur the Kid, mainly to himself, "isn't that strange?"

"Well, they must all be inside," said Seminole Maurice. "Come on, you three, start walking!"

They were about two hundred yards from the Wells, Fargo office when they began their slow and terrifying walk, Murderous B. Sutcliffe and Fat Phil each holding one of Arthur the Kid's hands, for all the world like any ordinary family taking a leisurely morning stroll, and Seminole Maurice bringing up the rear, a few yards behind, with the horses.

And then they were only a hundred and fifty yards away.

Arthur the Kid could feel the two hands holding his begin to tremble.

And then only a hundred.

And then fifty.

And

then

CRASH!

All four of them jumped! The sudden noise exploded on the silent street, and for a split second none of them knew what it was, and then they saw that it was no explosion at all but simply the double doors of the Wells, Fargo office being hurled back on their hinges with tremendous force and crashing against the building's walls.

After that, a moment later, four men backed out through the doorway. Two were dragging sacks, a third was pointing a shotgun inside the

office at what Arthur the Kid could now see
was a crowd of horrified faces, and the
fourth . . .

The fourth was holding a gun, too, but a six-
gun, in his right hand; and it was pointed at the
head of the little girl he was carrying under his
left arm.

The hands holding Arthur the Kid's suddenly
let go.

"They're robbing the Wells, Fargo office!"
gasped Murderous B. Sutcliffe.

"Shut up!" hissed Arthur the Kid, who was

suddenly as cold as ice inside, and thinking furiously.

"And they've got a little girl as hostage," whispered Fat Phil. "The rotten cowardly beasts!"

"Just keep walking slowly," said Arthur the Kid, very softly but very firmly; "just keep walking slowly toward them. They have no idea we're here." He walked on steadily as he talked. "They think they've got the whole town inside the office!"

The four robbers in front of them continued to back slowly away from the office, never taking their eyes (luckily for Arthur the Kid and his friends) off the prisoners inside.

"REMEMBER," roared one of the robbers, as he backed, "ANYONE MOVES AND THIS KID GETS BLOWN TO BITS!"

His voice was dark and ugly and full of evil, and even Arthur the Kid, bravest of the brave, could not help a chill shudder running through him, turning his stomach over. But it did not stop him for a moment, for he knew what he had to do, and what they all had to do, if the little girl was not to be killed or snatched away to heaven knew where. He walked on, knowing that there were just so many seconds left for him to make his move.

Then, suddenly, almost without realizing that he had done so, he made it.

From five yards away, sensing that the bandit holding the little girl was on the point of turning to dash for his horse, Arthur the Kid sprang, with all his strength, with all his agility, and with that very special spring for which all those mornings of very special exercises had prepared him, and he launched himself at the robber's back!

As he landed with his full force, he grabbed the robber's hair with one hand, while his other hand struck out at the man's gun arm; and such was the shock to the robber, this flying fighting weight from nowhere, that he dropped both his gun and the little girl in one astounded lurch!

As he pitched forward, the robber beside him with the shotgun whirled around at the noise. Arthur the Kid, still clinging to his victim's hair, caught a terrible picture in the corner of his eye of the twin wicked gun barrels swinging around toward him, and he thought, with a thought as quick and yet as clear and perfect as the flash of the picture, that this was a killer who would not think twice about firing, even if it meant killing his friend, too!

But in Arthur the Kid's ear, at that very same busy moment, burst the roar of a voice that was half familiar, yet, in its strange sharp toughness, half unfamiliar, too.

"DROP IT!" cried Fat Phil.

As he hit the ground, and rolled off and away from the man he had grabbed, Arthur the Kid looked up and saw Fat Phil in his pink flowered dress and pink frilly bonnet, and Murderous B. Sutcliffe in his green skirt and his yellow shawl, and they were both standing firm, with a revolver in each hand, and looking like anything but a pair of innocent old ladies.

Or, come to that, anything but a pair of pretty useless gunslingers.

Behind them, still on his horse, Seminole Maurice sat with his rifle up to his shoulder, trained on the two robbers with the sacks; and he didn't look like the sort of man who had spent his whole life fouling things up, either.

So the gang dropped their guns and their sacks, and slowly put their hands on their heads; and all of this had taken only about ten seconds.

In fact, it had all happened so quickly that the people trapped in the Wells, Fargo office still hadn't moved.

But then they did. Like some huge photograph suddenly coming to life, they unfroze and rushed outside, and cheered, and waved, and threw their hats in the air!

While the Wells, Fargo guards took hold of the four captured outlaws and hustled them away, the sheriff of the little town rushed over to Arthur the Kid, and helped him up, and dusted him off, and shook his hand, and exclaimed: "Why, you're a kid, you're just a kid! How did you, I mean, where did you, I mean, what did you . . . ?"

But before Arthur the Kid could answer or explain, they were both swept up in the cheering crowd, who had sat Seminole Maurice and Murderous B. Sutcliffe and Fat Phil on their shoulders, and carried off to the Fort Halleck Saloon, where everyone drank whiskey, except, of course, for Arthur the Kid.

When they had all calmed down a bit, the sheriff explained how the four men had ridden into town that morning, gone into one of the houses, and kidnapped the little daughter of the Wells, Fargo cashier; and how they had then gone from building to building, holding the little girl with a gun to her head and making everyone come out into the street, threatening to shoot her if they didn't. He told how they had then led everyone into the Wells, Fargo office, including the guards, who could naturally do nothing for fear of hurting the little girl; and how they had then forced the cashier to empty that day's gold shipment into their sacks.

"Which," said the sheriff at last, "leaves only one thing to be explained. And that's how you four happened to come along and rescue us!"

And Seminole Maurice and Murderous B. Sutcliffe and Fat Phil did not know what to say, so Arthur the Kid stepped in smartly, because he knew that if they did say something, it would be bound to be the wrong thing.

"Well," he said, "we're a gang that goes

around the country watching out for things, aren't we?"

The other three nodded; for it was true.

"And we're, well, pretty experienced in how easy it is for wicked men to break the law, right?"

They nodded again; for that was true, too.

"And we," continued Arthur the Kid, "had got to thinking about how easy it might be to spring a surprise on the Wells, Fargo office, just because everyone believed that nobody *dared* rob it."

"That's true," said Fat Phil. "We thought up this great . . ."

"So," said Arthur the Kid, loudly and quickly, in case Fat Phil went on to say something they might all regret, "we decided to come down here to see if it really was as tough to break into as everybody thought . . . and that's how we happened along."

Everybody cheered again, and nobody noticed the sigh of relief that Arthur the Kid breathed out; it hadn't been easy explaining things without telling a lie.

"Well, it's lucky for us you did," said a tall gray-haired man in a black frock coat. He smiled a broad smile. "And it's lucky for you, too. You've saved Wells, Fargo a hundred thousand dollars in gold today, and ten per cent of a hundred thousand is ten thousand, and that's what the reward is!"

There was a dull thud.

They had to drag Fat Phil out into the fresh air again, and put his head between his legs for the second time.

"Ten thousand dollars!" he gasped, when he came out of his faint.

"We'll never have to be outlaws again!" cried Murderous B. Sutcliffe. "We'll be able to sleep in beds, and eat regularly, and buy new hats, and . . ."

"Keep your voices down," said Arthur the Kid, as the three of them crouched there over poor Fat Phil, "and never even *speak* of being outlaws again!"

"We won't," said Seminole Maurice. "We always hated it, you know. I used to pretend, of course, just to keep everyone's spirits up; but I never thought it was right."

"I know that," said Arthur the Kid. "I knew that right away, and I realized I hadn't made a mistake when you saved my life just now, and the life of that little girl. You could have just ridden away."

"No, we couldn't," said Fat Phil, very firmly.

"That's what I mean," said Arthur the Kid.

A shadow fell across the group, and they looked up. It was the sheriff.

"There's just one thing puzzles me," he said,

"and that's why two of you gentlemen are wearing dresses."

Arthur the Kid stood up.

"There's some things," he said sternly, "which have to remain secret. For professional reasons."

"I understand," said the sheriff.

"I have to be going now," said Arthur the Kid. "Tell me, would I be right in thinking that that stagecoach passes through Laramie?"

"You would," said the sheriff.

"Then I think I'll hitch a lift," said Arthur the Kid.

He picked up his carpetbag, and he shook the hands of Seminole Maurice and Murderous B. Sutcliffe and Fat Phil. He walked quickly to the stage, and climbed aboard. The driver fired his pistol in the air, and the stage pulled out, on time and with the gold shipment safely stowed.

They watched it go, in a cloud of yellow dust, hurtling into the afternoon.

"I never even asked his name," said the sheriff.

72

Fat Phil pulled off his pink bonnet and wiped his eye with it.

"He was our boss," he said quietly. "He was Arthur the Kid."